# Muncha! Muncha! Muncha!

by

Candace Fleming

Illustrated by

G. Brian Karas

Atheneum Books for Young Readers

New York   London   Toronto   Sydney   Singapore

For Martha and Dan
—G. B. K.

To my muncha-muncha-
munching boys,
Scott and Michael
—C. F.

Atheneum Books for Young Readers
An imprint of Simon & Schuster Children's Publishing Division
1230 Avenue of the Americas
New York, New York 10020

Book design by Lee Wade

The text of this book is set in Kosmik.
The illustrations are rendered in gouache and acrylic with pencil.
Manufactured in China

Library of Congress Cataloging-in-Publication Data
Fleming, Candace.
Muncha! Muncha! Muncha! / by Candace Fleming. — 1st ed.
p. cm.
Summary: After planting the garden he has dreamed of
for years, Mr. McGreely tries to find a way to keep some
persistent bunnies from eating all his vegetables.
ISBN 0-689-83152-8
[1. Rabbits—Fiction. 2. Gardening—Fiction.] I. Title.
PZ7.F59936Mu 2001
[E]—dc21
99-24882

20  19  18  17  16  15  14  13  12

For years, Mr. McGreely dreamed of planting a garden. He dreamed of getting his hands dirty, of growing yummy vegetables, and of gobbling them all up.

But he never once tried it until—

"This spring!" said Mr. McGreely. "This spring, by golly,
I'm going to plant a garden."

So he hoed.

And he sowed.

And he watched his garden grow.

Lettuce!   Carrots!   Peas!   Tomatoes!
"Yum! Yum! Yummy!" said Mr. McGreely. "I'll soon
fill my tummy with crisp, fresh veggies."

But one night, when the sun went down and the moon came up, three hungry bunnies appeared.

Tippy—

Tippy—

Tippy,

Pat!

Muncha!

Muncha!

Muncha!

The next morning, when Mr. McGreely saw his gnawed sprouts,
he was angry.
So he built a small wire fence
all around his vegetable garden.

"There," he declared. "No bunnyscan get into my garden now!"

And the sun went down.
And the moon came up. And—

Tippy-tippy-
tippy,
Pat!

Spring-hurdle,
    Dash! Dash! Dash!

Muncha!

Muncha!

Muncha!

The next morning, when Mr. McGreely saw his nibbled leaves
and gnawed sprouts, he was really angry.
    So he built a tall wooden wall
        behind the small wire fence
        all around his vegetable garden.
    "Hmpf!" he huffed.
"Those flop-ears will
never get over it.
No bunny can get into
my garden now."

And the sun went down.
And the moon came up. And—

Tippy-
tippy-
tippy,
Pat!

Dig-scrabble,
Scratch! Scratch!
Scratch!

Spring-hurdle, Dash! Dash! Dash!

Muncha!

Muncha!

Muncha!

The next morning, when Mr. McGreely saw his chewed stems, his nibbled leaves, and his gnawed sprouts,

he was really, really angry.

So he made a deep wet trench,
     outside the tall wooden wall
     behind the small wire fence
     all around his vegetable garden.
"Hah!" he snorted. "Those puff-tails can't get under it. They can't get over it. No bunny can get into my garden now!"

And the sun went down. And the moon came up. And—

Tippy-tippy-
tippy,
        Pat!

Dive-paddle,
Splash!
Splash!
Splash!

Dig-scrabble,      Scratch!   Scratch!
Scratch!

Spring-hurdle,
Dash!   Dash!   Dash!

Muncha!

Muncha!

Muncha!

The next morning, when Mr. McGreely saw his chomped blossoms, his chewed stems, his nibbled leaves, and his gnawed sprouts, he was—

# FURIOUS!

So he hammered and blocked, sawed and stocked,
drilled and filled, and trapped and locked.
And he built a huge, enormous thing
before the deep wet trench
outside the tall wooden wall
behind the small wire fence
all around his vegetable garden.
"I've outsmarted those twitch-whiskers for sure,"
he exclaimed. "They can't get through it. They can't
get under it. And they can't get over it. No bunny, no
way, no how, can get into my vegetable garden now!"

And the sun went down.

And the moon came up. And—

# Tippy-tippy-tippy, STOP!

The three hungry bunnies looked and smelled and touched the huge, enormous thing before them. And—

# Tippy-tippy-tippy, pat.

The bunnies hopped away.

The next morning, when Mr. McGreely
saw his untouched vegetables, he was—

happy!

"I beat the bunnies!"
he whooped, and did
a jiggly, wiggly
victory dance.
    Then he—
        climbed over,
        jumped across,
        squeezed between,
        and crawled under until he reached his vegetable garden.
    "Ahh!" sighed Mr. McGreely. "At last!" Smacking his lips, he
picked and pulled up Lettuce! Carrots! Peas! Tomatoes! And with
his basket overflowing, he reached inside for something yummy.

Muncha!

Muncha!

Muncha!